Mr. Thomas and the Witch of Green Bay Pond

Elizabeth Thomas Holmes

Boot Publishing Inc.
14785 Preston Rd. Ste. 550
Dallas, TX 75254

Email address: bootpublishing@gmail.com

Visit us on our Web site @ www: bootpublishing.com

Graphic Design by: **Aneil Razvi**

Illustrations copyright © Boot Publishing 2016
ISBN-10: 069261172X
ISBN-13: 978-0692611722
Library of Congress Control Number:

Published by: Boot Publishing

Printed in the United States of America

Dedications

This book is affectionately dedicated to my daughter, Kelly Denise Thomas, my sibling, Beatrice, Christine, Patricia, William (June), Aaron Lee, Gary and Kevin I also dedicate this book to my readers and supporters. Thank you all.

Special Dedications
To those members of my family who are no longer with us

Mother: Lucille Harrell Thomas
Son: Leroy Thomas
Sister: Pearlie Mae Thomas Carruth
Brothers: Willie Frank,
Bruce Earl, Michael Ray and
Melvin Thomas

Acknowledgements

I humbly thank our Lord and Savior Jesus Christ for his love, mercy, grace and the strength given to me throughout my life.

"There is a time for everything, and a season for every activity under the heavens:" Ecclesiastes 3:1 (NIV)

A Note of Appreciations

Special appreciations goes to my sister, Jacqueline Marie Kelly Hollins, and my brother Henry Vincent Kelly as well as everyone involve with Boot Publishing Inc. that had a hand in helping this book to become a realization . Without your patience, kindness and love this children's book may have never been published. I hope this book will arouse the imagination of all the boys and girls around the globe as they journey with me through the pages of this book, Mr. Thomas and the Witch of Green Bay Pond

Travel through these pages to a place deep into the forest that will arouse your imagination in the world of Mr. Thomas.

Discover how his adventure leads him to a mysterious cabin deep into the forest where the Witch of Green Bay Pond dwells.

Once upon a time long, long ago, deep in the forest green, lived a logger named Mr. Thomas. Mr. Thomas lived with his wife, Wendy and their two small sons Kevin and William. As a logger, Mr. Thomas supported his family by going into the forest chopping down trees and selling them in the town nearby.

One night, after the children had been put to bed, Mr. Thomas said to his wife, "Wendy, the trees are getting very thin around here I must travel deeper into the forest to find good trees. The Mills in town require firm logs, and there just are not any good trees around here."

"Do as you must, my dear," said Mrs. Thomas, "but you must beware of Wanda, the Witch of Green Bay Pond."

"Very well," said Mr. Thomas, "I'll be careful. However, I must leave before the crack of dawn."

The following morning, Mr. Thomas was awakened by the smell of bacon frying on the Wood Stove. On the table sat homemade biscuits and maple syrup with a jar of fresh blueberry jam, his wife Wendy had preserved last spring.

After a hearty breakfast, Mr. Thomas and his family went out to the barn to prepare for his journey into the forest. While his sons hitched the horses to the wagon, he and his wife loaded the wagon with all the supplies he would need.

When the work was completed, he hugged his sons and kissed wife farewell. He was now ready to begin his journey, a journey that would take him deeper into the forest than he had ever dared to go before.

B_y the end of the third month, Wendy found herself worrying more than usual. Her husband had not yet returned and in her mind there was only one reason for his delay, "Wanda the Witch of Green Bay Pond."

To calm herself Wendy began to prepare supper, it was then she heard the excitement of her children's voices.

"Daddy! Daddy!" They shouted with joy, mom, daddy's home."

Out of the front door ran Wendy as she joined in the children's excitement. Her heart was filled with joy.

Mr. Thomas pulled the wagon to a stop. He's home and he's safe Wendy thought. Mr. Thomas hopped down from the wagon and he secured his wife and sons into his arms.

One month later, Mr. Thomas had to venture back into the forest, and once again, his wife reminded him to beware of Wanda the Witch.

"There are many dangers in the forest," she would say. "But, Wanda the Witch is the most dangerous of them all."

Mr. Thomas knew this to be true, because he too, grew up hearing the tales of Wanda the Witch. Not only did she hate the people who ventured into the forest, but she was known to be cruel to the poor little animals of the forest.

While chopping on a tree, Mr. Thomas had an eerie feeling that he was being watched. As he halted his axe, he looked around but saw nothing out of the ordinary.

As darkness drew near, Mr. Thomas packed his tools and headed back to where he had set up camp. He made a fire and from the back of the wagon he removed a basket of food his wife had prepared for him. After he ate, he unrolled his sleeping sack and while doing so, his thoughts drifted toward his wife and two sons. He felt guilty, because he wished he could spend more time with them.

There are lots of fine trees out here. He thought to himself. "If I make one more trip I should have sold enough lumber to last us until next summer, then I will be able to stay home and spend more time with my family."

That night, Mr. Thomas was wakened by the sound of a child crying. "I hear a child's cry," said Mr. Thomas as he stood to listen. "A child's cry is what I heard."

The crying became louder as he walked deeper into the forest in the direction of the child's voice.

He then came upon a clearing in the woods that he had not known was there. "A cabin," he exclaimed. "The crying is coming from the cabin."

As Mr. Thomas approached the cabin the door opened as if he had been expected. A woman stood in the doorway holding a crying child in her arms. Her hair was as black as coal without a strand out of place. Her dress was well worn but clean and her feet were bare.

"I heard the child crying, and I came to see if there is anything I could do to help" said, Mr. Thomas.

"Thank you kind sir, my name is Denise and this is my daughter Tramica. My husband left over seven weeks ago to buy food and milk, but has not yet returned. I'm afraid that something awful has happened to him. Now the baby cries for milk and I'm afraid we both will die of hunger if he does not return soon." Then she too began to cry.

"My dear lady, there is no need to cry," said Mr. Thomas. "Back at my camp I have enough food for you and your daughter. Tomorrow morning I will catch one of the wild she goats that feed near my camp each day, so that your daughter will have fresh milk."

As promised, Mr. Thomas returned to the cabin the next morning with the she goat, he also brought with him a sow and her litter of eight piglets.

It was then he noticed how different the cabin looked by daylight. The cabin had not been built by logs like other cabins. No, this cabin had been harshly put together with mud, twigs and dry leaves from the forest floor. Mr. Thomas had no idea how long the cabin had been standing, but what he did know was that it would not survive the winter.

He felt bad for Denise and her daughter. He knew he must help them. But, to do so meant he would have to leave the forest and return home to speak with his wife.

He decided to leave the forest and return home to speak with his wife immediately. Helping the Denise and her daughter meant more to him than the sales he would receive from the lumber.

Denise watched from the window as Mr. Thomas tied the she goat to a tree and made a makeshift pen for the sow and her eight baby piglets.

She opened the door as he was approaching and listened, as he voiced his concerns about her home not being able to survive the winter.

He then pointed to the she goat he had fetched for fresh milk and the sow and her litter of eight.

"You and your daughter should be ok until I return," he said." But, I must go now to speak with my wife."

They shook hands and Denise thanked him for everything he had done for her and Tramica. Mr. Thomas then left for his journey home.

When Mr. Thomas returned home he spoke to his wife about the woman Denise and her daughter Tramica who lived in the forest.

"You must bring them out of the forest at once," Wendy told her husband excitedly. "The witch of Green Bay Pond is sure to find them if they remain there."

Mr. Thomas nodded his head in agreement; he could see how worried his wife was regarding the safety of Denise and her baby, because he too shared her concerns.

"I will leave at daybreak," Mr. Thomas stated. "But now I must rest. The journey home has left me tired."

After a good night sleep Mr. Thomas started out early for his journey back into the forest. As he approached Denise's cabin of dirt, twigs and dry leaves from the forest floor, he went to her door and knocked, but he received no answer. He knocked again, but still there was no answer.

"My God," he whispered, "I hope nothing has happen to them." He then ran to the side of the cabin and peeped through an open window. From the sunlight shining into the room, he saw that the cabin was bare, as if no one had ever lived there. As he left the window, Mr. Thomas shook his head, he was confused. He had no idea where Denise and her baby could be.

"Hopefully they will find me if I make camp in the same place as I did before," he said to himself, as he left Denise's cabin.

J ust before dark, Mr. Thomas was having a sandwich by the camp fire when he spotted Mrs. Denise peering at him from beside a tree.

"My dear lady," he said excitedly. "How happy I am to see you. I thought something awful had happen to you."

As he approached where Denise was standing beside the tree Mr. Thomas was concerned as he asked, "Where is your daughter?"

"Behind me," Denise said, as she stepped aside.

How odd, thought Mr. Thomas as he saw the child sitting on the forest ground with a blade of grass hanging from between her teeth.

"The grass will do the child no harm," Mrs. Denise said with a sly smile as she saw the look of concern on Mr. Thomas' face.

"Mrs. Denise, I'm glad you have found me, with your approval I have come to take you and your daughter out of the forest," said Mr. Thomas.

"I could never thank you enough," replied Mrs. Denise. "But darkness has fallen and it is not wise to travel through the forest at night."

"This is true," replied Mr. Thomas. "We will leave in the morning. I have spoken to my wife about you and your daughter and she is looking forward to meeting the both of you." "I also cannot wait to meet her," replied Mrs. Denise. "My daughter and I must return to our cabin to retrieve a few items. We will be back here before sunrise. Then you may guide us out of the forest."

Mr. Thomas watched as Mrs. Denise picked up her daughter and disappeared into the darkness of the forest.

Later that night while Mr. Thomas was asleep Mrs. Denise was in her cabin with a large fire roaring in her fireplace. She had a huge black pot hanging over the fire, and as she stirred the bubbling brew within, she began to chant.

"The woodsman in the forest green,
And all my forest he had seen
my birds, my trees, my evergreen.
Those are things and they are mines.
This includes the waters of my
Green Bay Pond.
For the woods and all of this you see,
Yes, everything belongs to me."

As Mrs. Denise began to chant, the child crawled over to a corner in the cabin. Denise smiled a wicked smile as she walked toward the corner where the child was now staring up at her with wide eyes. Denise then pointed her boney finger at the child and chanted;

"For you, I have no more use, you see,
A rabbit once again you'll be."

The child then turned back into the beautiful white rabbit she once was and hopped happily out the door. Then Denise retuned back to her large black pot of boiling brew and continued to chant.

"No woodsman you will never go home. In these woods you will forever roam. A wolf, yes a wolf you will be and your wife and kids will hold the key.

For compassion and love they must show thee; if you ever wish to be free."

Mrs. Denise then threw something into the bubbling brew and a ball of blue flames rose out of it and hovered over the pot. She then began to laugh wildly as she continued her chant.

"These woods are home, yes, home to me. And there's no place I'd rather be. For I am Wanda the Witch you see.

As Wanda shouted the last of her chant the blue flames which hovered over the black pot exploded up the chimney and through the woods until it reached Mr. Thomas' camp. It then rested upon him as he slept.

When Mr. Thomas awakened the next morning he knew that something was not right. His face was too low to the ground and his hands and feet were that of an animal. He quickly dashed to the pond and looked into the water.

"A wolf, I've turned into a wolf." He said to himself as a mournful howl escaped his throat.

He then navigated his way through the forest to Mrs. Denise's cabin. But there was no cabin to be found. Only a small amount of mud and twigs remained. The wolf then began to howl his cry of frustration. Because now he was sure that the woman who called herself Denise was none other than Wanda the Witch of Green Bay Pond.

Time passed, days turned into weeks and weeks into months. Yet, no matter how much time passed Wendy hoped that her husband would one day return to her and his sons.

Kevin and William also believed their father would one day return. They enjoyed the liberty of being the men of the house. They fished and hunted for food and did not shy away from their chores. They knew if their father returned he would be proud of them. Because, the values that he had instilled in them, had not been forgotten. Mr. Thomas taught Kevin and William to listen to their mother and look out for each other.

But, most importantly Mr. Thomas taught his sons to respect the laws of the land and show love and compassion to all for God's creation.

Kevin and William were at the pond fishing, when they spotted a big grey wolf on the other side of the pond playing with a white rabbit. The boys laughed themselves silly as the rabbit leaped onto the wolf's back and the wolf began to run in circles in search of the rabbit.

When they returned home, the boys described what they had seen to their mother.

"There are no wolves that would venture this far out of the forest," she assured them.

"What you two might have seen was a wild dog in which case you need to be careful because they are known to be very dangerous."

The boys were certain of what they had seen, yet knew better than to disagree with their mother. So they both insisted that she return with them to the pond on the following day.

When morning came, Wendy packed a picnic basket for her sons. She was happy they had chosen her to tag along with them. By the time they reached the edge of the forest Kevin spotted the white rabbit.

"Look mom! The rabbit," said Kevin excitedly as he ran in the direction of the rabbit with his brother and mother following closely behind him.

"Something's wrong with it," remarked William as he watched the rabbit's strange behavior.

"Don't get to close, it might have rabies," warned Mrs. Thomas.

"No!" said Kevin, "I think it's trying to tell us something."

As if the rabbit had understood Kevin, she stopped leaping into the air and started hopping into the forest; however, she would stop every so often, to make sure that she was still being followed.

The rabbit led them to the clearing by a pond where a big grey wolf laid on his side whimpering in pain. Wendy cautiously approached the wolf to examine it. Yet, she found no sign that the wolf had not been harmed, neither could she find any signs that the wolf may have been caught in a hunter's trap.

Tears began to roll down Kevin and William's face as they remembered the wolf only a day ago running and jumping around as he played with the rabbit.

Mrs. Thomas saw the pain on her son's faces and the love and compassion for the wolf touched her where she also felt compassion. She reached down to stroke the wolf on his neck and their eyes locked.

"I know these eyes," she said, as the blue flames of Wanda the witches' spell lifted from the wolf and dispersed into the air.

"Jumping Catfish!" cried William, "Its dad!" Mr. Thomas suddenly felt better. He looked at his hands and saw that he was himself again. His family love and compassion had saved him. As a wolf he had been dying of a broken heart since he was unable to be with his family. Now that he was himself, he knew he would never leave his family side.

Before getting to his feet, Mr. Thomas picked up the rabbit, and with his wife on one side and his sons on the other; he led the way home where they all lived happily ever after.

THE END

Coming Soon in 2016

Keys to the Kingdom by Henry V. Kelly

ORDER FORM

Boot Publishing Inc.
14785 Preston Rd Ste. 550
Dallas, TX 75254

Name:_____

Address:_____

City:_____ State:_____ Zip:_____

Mr. Thomas and the Witch of Green Bay Pond $12.25

By: Elizabeth Thomas Holmes

Accepted forms of payment: Cashier Checks, Money Orders. Mail payment to address above payable to: Boot Publishing Inc.

For quick and easy method via PayPal, Credit Card for online order

Visit our website @ www: bootpublishing.com

Please allow 5-7 Business days for delivery.

----

www.ingramcontent.com/pod-product-compliance
Lightning Source LLC
Chambersburg PA
CBHW041753180626
46815CB00017B/25